A Note to Parents

Read to your child...

★ Reading aloud is one of the best ways to develop your child's love of reading. Older readers still love to hear stories!

★ Laughter is contagious! Read with feeling. Show your child that reading is fun.

★ Take time to answer questions your child may have about the story. Linger over pages that interest your child.

...and your child will read to you.

★ Do not correct every word your child misreads. Say, "Does that make sense? Let's try it again."

★ Praise your child as he progresses. Your encouraging words will build his confidence.

You can help your Level 2 reader.

★ Keep the reading experience interactive. Read part of a sentence, then ask your child to add the missing word.

★ Read the first part of a story, then ask your child, "What's going to happen next?"

★ Give clues to new words. Say, "This word begins with *b* and ends in *ake*, like *rake*, *take*, *lake*."

★ Ask your child to retell the story using her own words.

★ Use the five *W*s: WHO is the story about? WHAT happens? WHERE and WHEN does the story take place? WHY does it turn out the way it does?

Most of all, enjoy your reading time together!

—Bernice Cullinan, Ph.D.,
Professor of Reading, New York University

Reader's Digest Children's Books
Reader's Digest Road, Pleasantville, NY 10570-7000
Copyright © 1999 Reader's Digest Children's Publishing, Inc.
All rights reserved. Reader's Digest Children's Books and All-Star Readers are
trademarks and Reader's Digest is a registered trademark
of The Reader's Digest Association, Inc.
Fisher-Price trademarks are used under license from
Fisher-Price, Inc., a subsidiary of Mattel, Inc., East Aurora, NY 14052.
Printed in Hong Kong.
10 9 8 7 6 5 4 3 2 1

Library of Congress Cataloging-in-Publication Data

Kueffner, Sue.
    Lucky duck / by Sue Kueffner ; illustrated by Dana Regan.
        p.   cm. — (All-star readers. Level 2)
    Summary: When Emily gets a toy duck for her birthday, she thinks
it brings her good luck.
    ISBN 1-57584-309-9
    [1. Toys—Fiction. 2. Luck—Fiction. 3. Stories in rhyme.]
I. Regan, Dana, ill. II. Title. III. Series.
PZ8.3.K9447Lu   1999   [E]—dc21   99-19689

Lucky Duck

by Sue Kueffner
illustrated by Dana Regan

2
All-Star Readers™

Reader's Digest Children's Books™
Pleasantville, New York • Montréal, Québec

A box came for me
one day on a truck.

4

The kids ran outside.
They said, "Lucky Duck!"

I opened the box and what did I see?

Happy Birthday Emily!

A birthday surprise
from Grandma to me!

I love my small duck.
He goes where I go.

He's my
lucky duck.

And how do I know?

I took him to school
the very next day.

I got back my test—
and I got an A!

My mother had packed
my favorite treat.

Thanks to my duck,
I had good things to eat!

In art class, I drew
a perfect pink heart.

And in the school play,
I got the best part!

Yes, I was the star.
They made me Snow White.

My duck and I practiced
all day and all night.

I practiced my lines.
I soon knew them well.

But what if I tripped?
What if I fell?

The big night was here.
My duckie was gone!

The curtain went up!
How could I go on?

My teacher said,
"Emily, you will be fine.

You do not need luck.
You know every line!"

I went out that night,
and what do you know?

I was a hit!
The star of the show!

We walked home and talked about my big day.

Then Dad found my duck!
Thank you, Daddy! Hurray!

The play was a hit—
thanks to me, not my duck.

But getting him back?
Now THAT was good luck!

Words are fun!

Here are some simple activities you can do with a pencil, crayons, and a sheet of paper. You'll find the answers at the bottom of the page.

———————— ★ ————————

1. Match the scrambled words with the correctly spelled words on the right.

oxb	lucky
crutk	truck
clkuy	heart
lamsl	box
retha	small

2. Big words often have little words inside them. Cover some of the letters of each word with your fingers to see what little words you can find.

opened	birthday
tripped	teacher
outside	treat
heart	favorite

3. Match the words that rhyme—even though they may not be spelled the same way.

truck	show
white	fell
well	part
know	duck
line	night
heart	fine

4. Rearrange the words below to make a sentence.

drew   class   my   a

art   I   duck   in

5. Draw a picture of your special good luck charm, even if it's an imaginary one.

ANSWERS:
1. oxb=box, crutk=truck, clkuy=lucky, lamsl=small, retha=heart
2. opened: open, pen; tripped: trip, rip; outside: out, side; heart: he, hear, art; birthday: birth, day; teacher: tea, teach, each, ache, he, her; treat: eat, at; favorite: favor, or, it
3. truck/duck; white/night; well/fell; know/show; line/fine; heart/part
4. I drew a duck in my art class.